FAIE FABLES

Tales for Women

I0692355

written by Cherie Rence
illustrated by Cher Odum

COPPER WINGS PRESS

DEDICATIONS

To Bryan, for creating the space, the time, & the graphic design.
To my children, for insisting.
To Cher, for daring to dream with me.

Cherie Renae

To my daughter, for encouraging me to move to Oregon and pursue my art.
To the Bowers, for a cozy cabin where I can paint freely.
To Cherie, for being my vision keeper.

Cher Odum

ISBN 10: 0-6923-0320-0
ISBN-13: 978-0692303207

Copper Wings Press
Monmouth, OR 97361
www.copperwings.net

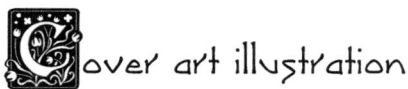

Cover art illustration

From the artist: We are the conductors of our own lives, and we can allow our souls to sing and dance. Make a joyful noise, and even the fish of the sea will play along!

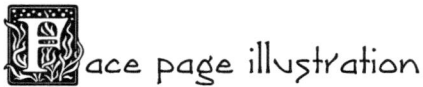

Face page illustration

From the artist: The water goddess was a journey within. One day, I deeply felt the pains of the past. I cried, I howled... and then I let go. A deep peace came over me, and the painting emerged. It represents the copious tears I shed that day, and the release of all the sadness.

Contents

Preface

My tales, like Cher's paintings, seem simple. But the more you look, the more you may see lying beneath the surface. We encourage you to explore your own perspectives - see the Postnotes for further thoughts and questions . Our wish is that these stories and art serve as starting blocks for your own adventures. Ready, set, go! --- Cherie

abulous Women

We're told
we're too stupid,
too smart,
too thin,
too fat.

We hear that
our feet are too big,
our bust is too small,
our dreams are too large,
our hips are too wide.

Worst of all,
we've told ourselves
these lies.

With these tales, I invite us to
 shout down our self-denigrating cries.
Here is the truth:
Women are fabulous
at every age and size!

From the artist: The pearl necklaces that my women wear represent pearls of wisdom. Through all of the good times, hard times, happy times and sad times, through all of the positive and negative stories that are told to us about our own worth, pearls of wisdom are gained. We share those pearls with others along the way.

Chosen Blindness

I heard a tale of a woman gone mad, a musician who tinkled the keys. One day, she burst from her home, took a stand in the street, and cried, "I can take this no more. Will a conductor like me, the board recommend me, a symphony hire me? I never know day to day. I'm worn down, deciding which bill to pay. It's too hard. I choose a different way." Then she went back inside.

Her friends whispered behind their hands, "We saw this coming long ago. Didn't we say, yes we did, you can't make money with music. It's not a true job, it's play. Now she'll learn what real work is, and labor 'til the end of each day."

They watched her house as they scurried off at eight o'clock prompt to shuffle their paperwork, text through their meetings, peek at Pinterest while the boss looked away. They watched her house as they stumbled home. But she didn't come out. "She's going to lose that house," they said. "How will she eat?" they said. "She needn't come running to us. She must help herself"

Then one day she emerged from her home, hands teeming with notes that tinkled and shone, and threw her arms high and wide. "Solomon in all his glory!"* sang the hymn of her heart. "Don't worry! Life is more than siding and apples and carpet and toast, more than sofas and blouses, more than blenders and boots."

Her neighbors ran into their homes, hands slammed over their ears, shouting to drown out the sound. Down the street she wandered, piano tucked under her arm. She was never heard from again.

"See, that's what happens when you follow strange yearnings," said parent to child. "Be realistic, not fanciful. Be practical. Learn how to frown."

But they say in a beach town, miles away, a woman appeared dressed in sheets of sound, playing piano in time with the tides. With each swell, her harmony rose, with each ebb, a haunting refrain. Strangest of all, they said, was the scarf that covered her eyes, chosen blindness to shut out the lies.

*reference: Matthew 6:25-34

The Listener

Maha sat still as a spider at the foot of the couch and listened as the men spoke of jobs and the weather, of war and its hell, of the time that beer spewed out of Da's nose when Uncle Jimmy stepped on the cat's tail. The cat was fine. Uncle's leg was not.

Maha giggled aloud. She should have kept silent, for Da heard and turned his head, his large sun-browned forehead wrinkling. He said, "Don't be lazy. Get up. Help your mama! There's work to be done while that sun's in the sky."

Maha sighed. That meant dishes, washing and drying and putting away. But if she was careful and quiet, she might hear her mother and aunt at their gossip as they hung the clothes on the line. She stood at the sink, and leaned toward the sill as they whispered outside.

"He's no good, my Jimmy," said her Aunt Margaret Mae. "He buys jewelry and dresses for that strumpet of his. I get dish soap and floor wax."

Mama replied, "Well, at least your house is sparkling clean." And they laughed.

"He brought me roses 'to brighten the place.' He said that my scowling was making it dim. If I had a petal for each time that man strayed, I'd be floating in flowers," Auntie said leaping, jiggling arms upraised, before landing, thunk, on the ground.

"What you gonna do," said Mama. "If you don't laugh, you'll cry."

As years tumbled by, Maha nurtured an extravagant garden filled with redolent blossom. She grew roses and daisies, foxglove and mum. She walked through the cosmos, and smiled in the sun. Men came aplenty with little limp handfuls of wilted arrangements, sure a wink and their nosegay would win them a smile. But Maha just shook her head.

One day came a man with hands empty but willing. He picked up a shovel, bent his back to his work. He tilled a new bed, then pulled seed from his pocket, sprinkled it and tamped it down tight. He returned every day to water and wait. His attention caused the flowers to flourish. They grew tall, raising their heads to the sky.

"These are for you," said the man, observing Maha's open-mouthed wonder. "They stand tall on their own, they look to the sun, and their beauty is unsurpassed. Just like you. May I work at your side?"

Maha put her ear to his heart. She liked what she heard. She looked in his eyes and nodded. The man smiled, for Maha wasn't the only one who listened.

From the artist: I paint many spirals into my works as a reminder that life never ends. Even in dying, we are reborn. The spiral also represents the curl of the wave, the lift of the wind, the umbilical cord. It represents life!

From the artist: White is purity and simplicity. It is a reminder for me to keep things simple and easy. White is the blank canvas waiting for me to paint my story on it. White invites the words and the color . . . and the messages from my soul The flowing hair in my works represents our need sometimes to go with the flow

Broken Bubbles

Kira's legs stay together to avoid chance mistake, and she hunches to hide her small breasts. It does no good, boys still whistle, causing Mother to lecture again. Don't look over! Cross your arms! Cross your legs, do you want them to see?

Her shoes are too tight. No, your feet are too big, says mother, frowning again. You won't marry if you don't hide those huge boats. Put that book down! Quit thinking! No one wants a smart girl. Watch TV, knit a vest, try to smile, not too broad, do you want them to think that you're cheap?

Kira cowers and she bows but there's no place to hide. In her bubble, she's hopelessly trapped. Trotted out, put away, held tight in clawed hands, 'til a day when, caught by a need for fresh air, Mother stalks to the shore. At a cliff by the sea, Mother raises the bubble, but the breeze whips the bauble, which slips through her fingers and lands in the waves. Mother screams, Mother shouts. Don't let her get away! There's no telling what she'll do or where she'll go if I don't keep control! Make her stay!

But this is the moment for which Kira's prayed. She stretches her arms, pops the bubble, smiles wide, grows fins and a tail, and swims quickly away with the tide.

Today Kira reads as much as she likes on a sun-warmed rock in the surf. Boys still whistle, but she's no longer shy. Shoulders back, she smiles and she waves. Her mother stands yet at the edge of the sea, squawking, shame, shame, living under the sky!

Life is not a house, but a heart. Sand and sea, shells and books are more than enough, she hears the mermaid reply.

From the artist: Music makes my soul dance. Music lifts my spirits when I slip into that mode of self-doubt. When I dance, it lifts my vibration. I imagine that joyful vibration going out through the world and touching all of the souls who are feeling down, and in turn lifting their vibration. That's why all of my fish are dancing. When we raise our vibration to those higher levels, even the fish dance.

Always Leaving, But Never Gone

He's left her, again. Sarah wants to howl at the moon, but she fears she'll never stop. Instead, she reaches to the back of a packed linen shelf and extracts a small case abandoned since high school. She flips the hinges, lifts the lid, then sucks on a reed as she assembles the horn. Holding it close, she marches into the orb-lit night and squeaks and squawks her frustration.

Six months later, he texts as though no time has passed. She tries to hold righteous anger as a rigid barrier against his fickle heart, but an earthen dam has no chance against passion's flood. He has a better job now, he says. He's learned the salsa, read Alice Hoffman, and downloaded Mishka's albums. He stays longer this time, disappearing with promises of a grounded return. "I will learn to love you better," he says, slinking away.

Once again, her licorice stick is her salvation, her solace, her love, singing her through the long, sleepless nights. She carries it camping, held in her lap as she sits by a stream on the cool, stilling earth.

Watching the river rush from the moon's sparkling love, spread so carelessly across the waters, Sarah wonders, why are both river and man so eager to flee? What's the rush to escape? It's so like them both to leave a wet mess as they evaporate around the bend, never gone but always leaving.

She lifts her horn and exhales her heartbreak with the throaty sobs of love gained and love lost, harsh music to fill the night. Bay loudly, sister Sarah! In your inchoate cries, we hear truth and lies, frothing chaos that covers, that smothers, that fills all the cracks in our heart-rending lives.

What Dreams Are Left

What shall I take, she ponders, leaning against her iris-blue truck, its new car musk contrasting with nature's rich bloom. Nothing, she realizes: neither license nor passport, for she needs no identity here. Swiping dirt from her sweater, she checks her long laces, cords noose-tight, before starting her slow climb.

At the top of the bluff, she sits against a fallen tree, gazing across a valley toward mountains whose shoulders are rounded like those of a long-married man.

I'd be your wife, she thinks. I'd marry you with your eroded edges, pikes scuffed smooth by storms beyond memory's reach, no prickly points or jagged rims to rend tender flesh. You'd unleash upon me no displaced ire from your trysts with glacial beauties of ages gone by, because you understand that icecaps ablate, floodwaters result, and then parts of you tumble away. You don't yearn for the boulders that were, but appreciate the beauty of a moraine-strewn valley, dewy in the sparkling dawn. I'd marry you, yes, I would, for if too much of you has been ground away, better that than a young crag whose caustic contours scrape and scar.

You know how it feels to mourn the eons-slow ebb of mountainous passion, for you watched helpless as the continent slowly slid by, severing you from your molten roots. Did you feel impotent rage when Terra ground her Gaia-wide hips against fresh soil? Did you resent the resultant uplift and eruptive birth of new peaks, straining red against the blue sky? She imagines the mountain turning away, not watching, before finally falling asleep. Do you still dream? she wonders. Do I?

I've lived almost as many years as you. I've outlived one husband, two children, six dogs, twenty cats and a turtle - though the turtle didn't die, it just wandered away some forty years past, and is probably living still. What dreams are left for those as ancient as we?

But Santiago still dreamed of his lions.* Men, even old, have a place in their soul that roars. They won't just lie down like this vast mountain range, no, they growl and they hiss 'til they die. She's watched them rattle their Ezekiel bones. She's lifted their bodies, damp with the strain of expiring; she's soothed their sick flesh with fresh sheets and soft kisses. Now her skeletal hands lie trembling in her lap. They've wiped their last brow. They've stroked their last cheek.

The time that's left is mine, just mine, she whispers to the purpling peaks. I've lived many places, but not all, there are corners yet for me to explore. And I will. But for now, this seems like a good place to rest.

*reference: Ernest Hemingway. The Old Man and the Sea.

From the artist: Her purple hair signifies spiritual enlightenment. She felt beaten down in the city, so she's put it behind her, at least for a while. She's counting her lucky stars - thankful that she still has hope!

From the artist: Green is for growth and abundance. Abundance isn't always financial or material, but often times seen in our friendships and families. It is also indicates spiritual growth. Red is for passion. What are YOU passionate about?

Dragonfly Dreams

Anya slipped outside as birds chirped farewell to the evening sun. A cerise dragonfly flittered through the last glint of light shining between two trees. Dragonflies, night-blind despite eyes that boast 30,000 lenses, are easy prey for bats and owls, and this one was flying late. "Hurry home, water dipper," Anya called.

It did not, in fact, hurry. It hovered iridescent in the sun's final ray, sparkling like a ruby. Anya stepped closer. It buzzed an ellipsis about her head, stopping a few feet away. "What do you want?" she laughed.

The clouds blazed bittersweet as the sun slipped below the horizon. "You're going to be dinner if you don't find a warm rock for the night," she said sternly. The dragonfly zipped toward her and back. "Fine, I'll humor you." She stepped forward.

I'm humoring myself, she thought. Are you so lonely you imagine interactions with insects? She walked across the lawn, following the dragonfly to the creek that bordered her yard, eager for mystic connection. But when they arrived, it zipped away, joining its black brothers on a large stone. See, thought Anya, you imagined something where there was nothing. You always do.

She sat on the stream bank, peeled off her shoes, sank her toes into the water and sighed. A sigh can mean many things. This was the sigh of decisions regretted and choices not made. The red dragonfly, wooed by the smell of berry-sweet breath, arose and lit on her shoulder. "Is it too late?" she asked. "When a dream passes by a soul frozen in fear, does it ever return again?"

The dragonfly rose, nipped the bridge of her nose, and returned to its rock for night's slumber. But his lovebug nip opened her one-lensed eyes, and for the first time in years, she saw. Dreams filled the brook before her! "We're not allocated just one wish a life. There are hundreds from which we can choose. I could have jumped in any time. I still can."

The dragonfly heard a laugh and a splash. Anya surfaced, fingers filled with desires, tossed her wet hair, and swam.

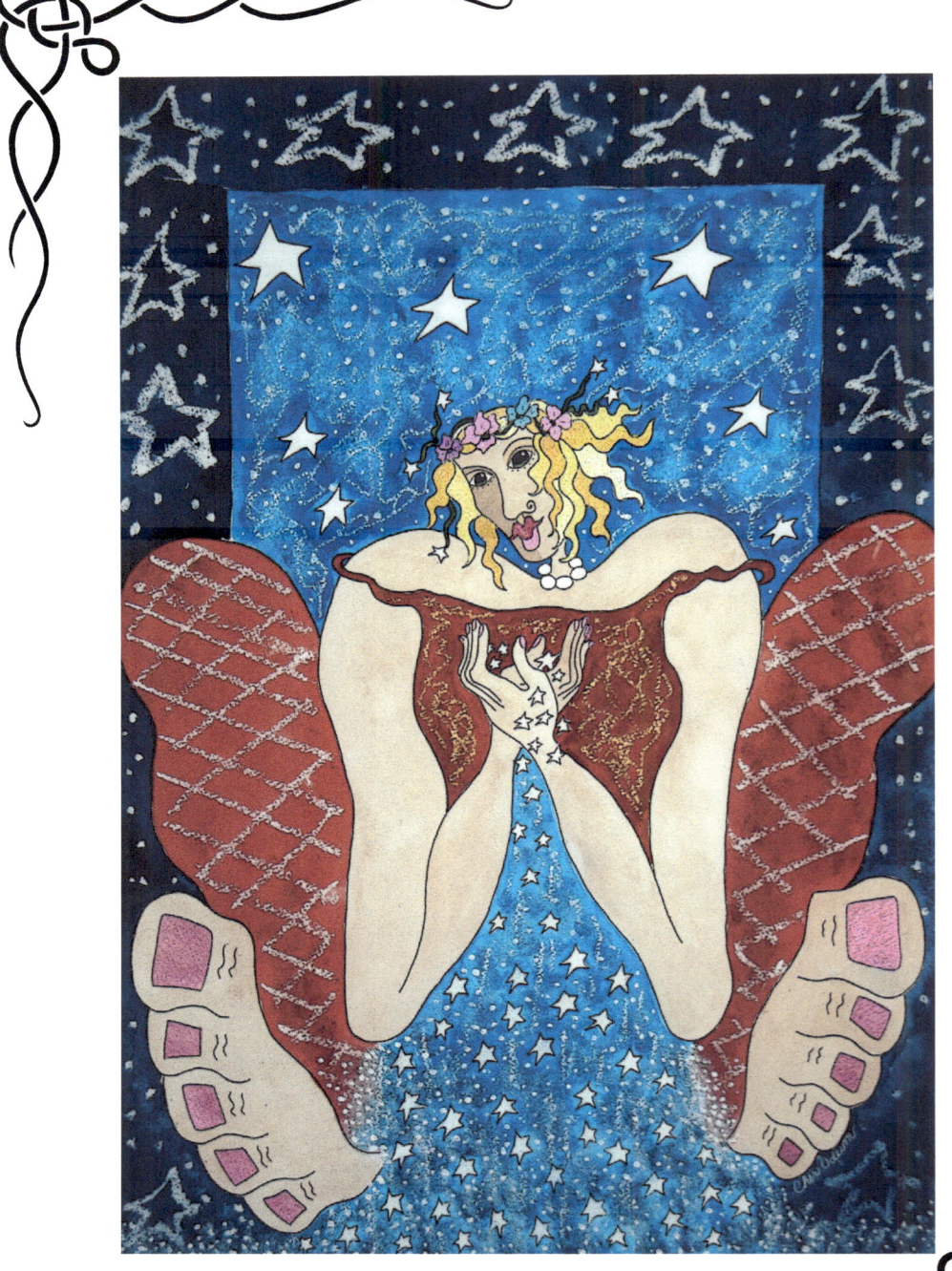

From the artist: Stars represent hope and wishes fulfilled: wishing upon a star like we did when we were children and believing our wishes will come true. They're a reminder to be more childlike in how we view and walk through this world.

Woven Words

Words tumble out Nora's mouth, numerous as stars in the sky. She chitters of flowers and trees, of love and of joy. "Can't you stifle yourself?" asks her husband, irritation wroth on his face. But she can't turn it off, there's just too much to share. She tries to stem the tide of tales, shoving her fist in her mouth to stop the flow. But then she spies the petals of a rose freshly bloomed, and words tumble out, coral and velvet to fragrance the ears.

"Jeez, Mom, you're embarrassing me," says her daughter, ducking out the front door. "Don't mind my mom," she says to her friends, "she never knows when to shut up."

Nora cries. She watches the door. Today when they come, she will learn to be quiet, be seen and not heard. She doesn't want to embarrass, doesn't want to annoy. It's just that there's dew on the grass and moss in the trees; verdant visions demand to burst forth from her soul, and the only path out is through words. She retreats to her room. Perhaps she can talk herself out while they're gone.

Nora's quiet when they return. In silence, she serves them their meal. She gathers the leftovers, cleans the table, kisses the children and nods to her spouse. She goes to her room and closes the door. They're relieved. Without Nora's chattering, they can hear the TV.

It happens again the next night, and the next. "What's the matter, cat's got your tongue?" mocks her husband, uneasy with change. She smiles and nods, but she shares not a word. She holds tight her tongue when there's someone to hear. Only when she's alone does she loose the beauty that's held in her heart. She weaves it around her, a beautiful quilt.

One day, her family returns to a home silent of scent and of movement as well as of sound. There's no dinner, no light except a strange twinkling from under Mom's door. They open it. Nora leans out the window, arms raised high, wrapped in a blanket that looks like the sky. They gasp. Is this really their wife and their mother? They gaze at her beauty, see her soul dancing bright, but she sees only the stars in her eyes.

Filmishmish

Filmishmish is a Lebanese phrase. Literally, it means 'during apricot season', which is very short, thus figuratively it means that something is unlikely to occur.

They certainly weren't sisters, they weren't even friends. The three women arrived early each morning with baskets of season-ripe fruit. Jamilie's dates were sticky and sweet. Latifeh's pomegranates promised esurient sin, while Aniese's apricots whispered filmishmish again. Women flocked to their tables, frowning and pinching despite pleas to desist, buying tree-sweet indulgences they couldn't resist.

Aniese was single. No husband, no lover, disturbed her repose. She emptied her basket, tucked her earned silver away, then returned to her cabin at the end of each day, where she chopped her own wood and read novels by the fire's flickering light. She needed no one, she thought, she wanted no friends. Loneliness was better than the cycle of fights and amends.

Jamilie was married, but her husband brought no delight. She reveled instead in town gossip, ripened fresh in the town square on warm Virgo nights. She savored each morsel of insinuatory fig, juice of its gossip dripping down past her chin.

Latifeh, ah Latifeh, dreamed of worlds far beyond. Her lover, Anna of the soft thighs, wove visions of the divine before Latifeh's awed eyes. They spoke reverently of the Prophet, of his wife and his son, their cuddled bedchamber filled with dreams of a peace yet unwon.

Aniese and Latifeh upset Jamilie. Was it not enough to vie with other women for her husband's attention, must she vie for customers, too? So she slandered them in the village. "Aniese, unmarried? How disgraceful, it's long past time!" she sighed in the evening over her unwatered wine. "And Latifeh and Anna? It's wrong in Allah's sight." Her words carried back to the women. Latifeh cried in Anna's arms, but Aniese thought, "People are treacherous. I was right."

One morning, Jamilie failed to appear. Aniese and Latifeh knew that without Jamilie's hostile glances, they could sell without fear. But it wasn't Latifeh's way, "What would the Prophet say?" Aniese, after thought, followed her to Jamilie's home, where they found her sick and alone. Her husband had long since departed; she'd woven fanciful stories to explain why he was gone. They bathed her brow, held her hand, fed her fruit from their baskets and clucked at her groans.

Jamilie recovered, but her tongue was never the same. It refused to waggle, becoming quite tame.

They certainly weren't sisters, but perhaps they were friends. They arrived each morning with baskets of season-ripe fruit: dates sticky and sweet; pomegranates promising esurient sin; apricots whispering filmishmish again. Though apricot season may last only a blink, we should never forget it's a Divine wink. Miracles happen, filmishmish indeed, when we heed Allah's nudge and help those in need.

From the artist: When I painted these women I was contemplating the connection between body, mind and spirit, as well as the connection between every living thing. Separateness is an illusion; we are all one on a universal level.

From the artist: Blue represents calm, and it feel like a hug from the Universe. The water in my paintings represents our emotions, and the need for us to tune in to ourselves and listen. How soothing it is, and easy to tune in while walking on a beach, or sitting and listening to the surf.

The Garden

He couldn't conceive of a musical thing. He didn't lack acumen, he had brains quite sufficient, but he suffered a paucity of imaginative thought. Passionate about the flora and fauna, he felt the garden was wonder enough.

But Khavah grew tired of pruning the tender limbs, cleaning up goat dung, and shooing chickens from out of the grove. Her heart didn't sing, it groaned. And as she thought this, she wondered "What is 'sing'?" She felt it might be sound, and sure enough, it was. But her melody was lonely without harmony, so she took some sticks and snake skins, cut them into thin little strips, and soon she fashioned a beautiful harp.

Her music crooned of heavenly wisdom, of visions beyond the stars. The harp was a portal twixt there and here, and soon Khavah's eyes were opened to what lay beyond. She sang to Adamah, whose ear became jealous. Who was she, mere woman, to sing of such things?

He grabbed her harp. "You don't need this vile tool! Trees and snake strings don't peal forth with truth! You shouldn't sing of what you don't know." Then he smashed her creation.

Khavah cried, and her wailing brought down the Divine, who said, "Adamah, what is this?"

Adamah sputtered in rage, "The woman, the tree limbs, the snake strings, the song. The woman you gave me! This isn't my fault. It's just wrong."

Divine whispered gently, "Adamah, you've hurt her. How do you plea?"

Adamah jutted his jaw and hardened his heart. "This isn't my doing. I refuse to repent. If there's blame to distribute, I point it your way. You made her beguiling, her mouth filled with fanciful words."

This was too much, even for a patient Divine. "Leave the garden, you ignorant fool. Go sit on the hard ground outside the gate. Leave her alone."

But Khavah loved Adamah. "No, Great One, I'll go with him, lest he pine away. He loves the trees and the flowers, the birds and the beasts. He'll listen if I sing reason to him."

But Adamah continued to call it all lies. He told a new story and died, still unwise. Khavah taught her daughters to sing and to play, which they do to this day, endlessly wooing Adamah's sons to return to the Garden, to love and enlightenment, to the outstretched arms of the Divine.

Birdie Whispers

Birdie whispers in my ear. I should grow wings and fly away, but instead I stay and listen. I can't resist, for she brings the juiciest worms. When we've finished our feeding frenzy, she waddles away. I watch her and wonder, why doesn't she fly? Her sparrow-like hops are heavy, as though she's still laden, though she unburdened herself on me. I squint to spy a hidden restraint, but there's nothing that I can see. What weighs her down?

Well, it's none of my concern, though I mention it to Laynie Jane that evening as I hand her a drink. "That Birdie. Her flitting tongue never stops, but who is she to talk of other's faults? She's plenty of her own. I heard she has a daughter at college who's turned up pregnant, a delinquent son, a husband who's out of a job. I heard he drinks and beats them all."

She replied, "Oh, Birdie's got no room to talk. Last week when she told me of Audrey's plight - another child and at her age, too? Birdie says it belongs to that handyman, Ted. Anyway, she said not a word of her daughter's misdeeds, though I hinted I'd heard someone else has a bat in the cave. She thought it was you! ... is it true? You can tell me, you know. I won't breathe a word. Hey! Watch it! There's no need to spit!"

I splutter and choke as I fume, "She said WHAT? You know that's not so. I can't believe you'd listen to that! Looks like what she said about you is true."

Silence. Then with French horn lips, she asks, "And what exactly is said of me?"

Thus, the evening unravels and our friendship frays away. Next morning, Birdie whispers in my ear. I should grow wings and fly away, but instead I talk and I talk. She coos and she clucks, she listens and sighs, and then she waddles away.

From the artist: The woman is pointing toward herself. It suggests that we all create our own fate, our own reality. The bird represents her inner voice, her intuition. We too often listen to the outside world, but the answers to our questions lie within us.

From the artist: I use blindfolds to express how we use our intuition. For example, the chemistry between these two is palpable. They don't need to see each other to feel each other's energy. They have a spiritual and chemical connection that transcends sight and other physical senses.

Clandestine Love

Sandra knows she should have plucked this perfidious plant when first it sprang through the edge of her lawn. She smiles as watches its salacious leaves salute the sun, stalks wiggling an herbaceous lap dance of love. But it's rooted in an inappropriate place. What would the neighbors say? With a sigh, she stiffens her shoulders and snatches the shears with resolute hand. Walking to where the wayward weed dances, she flexes her arms - and pauses. It's so pleasing in its own wild way. Perhaps, Sandra thinks, she can prune it into propriety.

Decorum has been her safe domain, but suddenly she feels chained. Her face flushes. What is proper? Are sculpted hedges and crosshatch lawns truly seemly, or are they indecent attempts to tame natural growth? Is it perhaps not modesty, but pomposity that keeps her from humming along with the bees as they snatch sacred honey from a flower's private place?

In the end, Sandra lets the weed stand, knowing it will root deeper than she suspects, knowing it will take over, making a mess of her manicured plans. But it's beautiful as it sways seductively in the summer breeze with whispers of invitation and she, fecund soil, receptive to seed, is inexorably drawn. The shears fall from Sandra's hand as her hips begin to move in time with her heartbreak and hallelujah weed.

Single-Fingered Salute

Arthritic ankles crossed, Angela sips coffee at a sidewalk café. Watches the drama unfold from the yarn store across the way as young women, arms filled with new-found fiber, charge out and dodge through screeching cars. Saddle up their metallic mounts. Dig their spurs in. Join the race.

Angela's mind is stuffed with memory's wool, of her own youthful hands and busy feet. Knit one, stitch two, business school. Cast on, accounting. Paying bills. Children's lessons, concerts, college. House. Car. A new TV. Another. Bigger. Another. Better. Another. This time, with HD.

Vacations when the kids are grown. Branson: boring. Husband loves it. Nashville. Ditto. Cue vacations: exit right. Husband melts into his chair, both with bursting seams. His fingers slow, their channel-flipping frenzy fading. Knit one, purl two, casting off, and now an empty stage.

Today she sits, no need to rush. Her age-stiff back is rigid, middle finger of the ancient set. She smiles as the puerile crowd looks right through her, sure her knitting days are done. Defiantly she reaches down, extracts fandango fleece and needles from her haversack. Slip knot, loop, casting on. Knit two, purl one - an endless row - for Angela has many stitches yet to go.

From the artist: This woman is wool-gathering: contemplating all who have come and gone. The knitting represents a peaceful, loving life. The yellow-orange umbrella symbolizes the chakras that deal with personal power and emotional growth.

From the artist: The umbrella is a shield against emotions; she is trying to avoid dealing with the bear. The bear represents death and perhaps resurrection, while the rabbit depicts her fear, timidity and nervousness. Finally, there is the frog, who offers hope for change and renewal

Amphibious Perspective

A stranger appeared at the end of a very long day. You'll do," he said. "Your mouth is too broad but your fingers are long. You're not a looker, but you'll do." I pretended that he meant no offense and I went with him, lured by sunshine, dreams, and a promise to play.

It's not what I hoped. He drinks until he's no longer himself, dancing as though he's just discovered two legs. "Hey! Where's my umbrella?" he roars. "A drink should have one, dumb bunny. So should I -" here he pauses to view the clear sky "- just watch those grey clouds gather!"

I shiver. I, too, sense a storm coming, when thunder will roll. So I keep my eye open; it's likely to start when I croak the wrong tune. I'm ready to hop to the hills. If it rains hard enough, perhaps I can swim.

Desert Mother

I abhor the places where boisterous folk cluster, their words swarming like ants atop one another, a black heaving hill where individual meaning is lost. "It's how people ARE," they proclaim. They wrap me up in their corporate arms with a hug that's too hard and guffaws that cause my ears to ring. "Come in! It's polite! It's expected!"

I've mastered the sincere smile. Affixing it firmly onto my face, I slide slowly away from the center, away from the noise and the crush. I've read the self-help books. I know that balance comes from within, not without, and I should be strong and able to hold my heart in harmony even when chaos reigns.

But I can't. I don't. So I flee away to the lonely lands, where I can hear when the transmundane whispers - in the sky, in the hills, in the music I birth, divine fire flaming forth, though too soon extinguished, its moisture sucked into parched earth.

All withers without the water of life. So I hold forth a hazel twig. It points not thither, not yon, not up nor down, but straight at my belly. Right here, deep within, lies an ebullient brook to lubricate the river of notes, notes to nourish, revive, notes to sooth those who strive, notes that woo seekers who gather and join in terrestrial hymns.

There's an ocean in the desert, and I was called to seek it. I'm alone, not withdrawn, I'm surrounded by sound. I'm immersed in color, in water, in flame. I'm alive!

From the artist: The pink balls represent childlike joy. Orange is hope, generosity and a giving nature. The desert offers unlimited access to the universe. The quail promises we can overcome our limitations, and the snail gives us permission to go at our own pace.

All Together Now

Two women sipped sake. One sat in shadow, the other in the setting sun's glow. The first said, "We see what we want to see, but it's not real. There's no 'real'. We each live in a fantasy that we think is reality, but it's illusion, it's just all mist."

The second replied, "Oh, my friend, don't be glum. Real is what our hearts sing. Real is what we feel when we clasp hands and dance. Real is the kinship of all creation. We're connected to the trees and the stars, to the stones and the snails, to each other. That's real."

The first was encouraged, so the second scribed her words, or perhaps she committed them to paint. For you see, this conversation truly happened; it occurred between Cher and Cherie.

Who was who? Well, it depends on the day. We - all of us - live in a seesaw world, one up while another is down. It's easy to imagine we're alone in the gloaming, when the world slips into the night. But if we remember we're all in this together, then we create a cosmos where a body builder becomes a painter, a mystic writes a song, a daughter finds freedom and fins. We can choose a new Eden, a new story. We can clasp hands together and dream.

From the artist: I use fun color and joyful movement to help us remember we are all beings of pure light and love. Our stories matter. We are beautiful women, we are abundant women. We have so much to share with the world!

AFTERWORD

They didn't know what to do with me at Pacific University, where I completed my MFA in Writing. I didn't know what to do with me, either. The other fiction students wrote of grit and blood, of heartache and death. They wrote sensible prose that stayed solidly on the page.

I, on the other hand, wrote mystical yaw. A weed became a lover; a mountain, a spouse. My fiction started dancing, then rhyming. As you can see, it still does. But it's not poetry, not quite. It lives in the hinterland twixt prose and poem. It lives half in what's real, and half in...well, what's also real, just not here. I mean, what is fiction, really? Aren't all stories true somewhere?

Cher's paintings are the perfect accompaniment to my prosetry. Or perhaps my words attend her art. Either way, we inspire each other. We've talked for years of doing a joint project, and I'm tickled we finally met in the crossroads to complete this book. Perhaps another will join it someday.

These tales arose from my experiences and those of women around me. Our stories are common, full of heartache and hurt, but also humor and love. Fulfillment — that elusive 'happily ever after' - is there for us if we are willing to let loose society's false straps, shush our inner naysayer and step boldly along the path of our dreams.

My thanks to Dave Calhoun for his editorial eagle eye. Thanks also to Miriam Haugen and Christie Hendersen for our wine-fueled brainstorming session, which led to many of the story titles.

--Cherie Renae, October 9, 2014

Postnotes:
An Opportunity to Engage

Here are additional thoughts about each of the pieces. I've included questions for those who would like to further engage either individually or as a group.

hosen Blindness

I'm surprised how many people think the life of a full-time artist is purely idyllic. In their minds, we do nothing but sit around all day, paintbrush, camera or keyboard in hand, allowing the sweet breeze of creative inspiration to carry us along as money pours in the door. (Though they do think, privately, that we charge a bit *too* much for our painting, print or poem.)

An acquaintance once said, "It's like being retired, isn't it? You only work when you want to." Well, yes. As long as I want to work long hours. LONG hours. I'm a one-woman shop, the cash flow is variable, and it's hard! Like many (most) artists, I sometimes spend sleepless nights worrying about the basics of life — housing, health insurance, food. Worries my acquaintance, with her government job, doesn't experience or understand.

The solution is obvious, right? Go get a *real* job. Practically speaking, no one should choose art as a profession. And that's why most talented people do take other paths, consigning their artistic expressions to hobby status. I applaud them. I often envy them. In fact, I used to BE them.

For years, I worked in corporate America. Lucrative professional positions. Job security and great benefits. But then my husband died. I was torn from my comfortable world, torn from myself. When I finally found my way back and stuffed myself into the hole that was me, I must have crawled in backwards, because things looked very different. I tried to go back to what I'd been, but the path — and the person — was gone.

So here I am. I'm an artist because I can't not be.

1. What art forms speak to you? (Consider music, visual art, tactile art, written word, and all forms of creative expression.)

2. Does it benefit a community to have full-time artists? Why or why not?

The Listener

As a girl, I was like Maha. Running outside with my cousins wasn't nearly as interesting as listening to the adults, who spoke of about life in the old country and politics in the new. I especially loved listening to my grandfather's war stories. An American citizen who emigrated from Syria, he loved his adopted country and volunteered when the Great War broke out. He was assigned to the cavalry who patrolled the Texas border, searching for some outlaw. I was spellbound as he spoke of saddle sores and river bathing, of horses and whiskey, of friendship and death.

It wasn't just stories of the war. Gidu spoke of his childhood as an orphan, his boat ride to the new world, his adventures and sorrows. After his death, people called the world around, and everyone remembered his stories. My ability to spin a tale comes from the greatest storyteller, my Gidu.

Oh, and it wasn't until I was grown that I realized who he was seeking on our southernmost border. My grandfather hunted Pancho Villa! Imagine.

1. Margaret Mae laughed to hide her broken heart. Maha kept hers out of reach. Whose way, if either, was healthy?

2. How do you react to negative circumstance?

Broken Bubbles

"No one likes a smart girl." "No one will marry a fat girl." These were messages I absorbed as I grew up, and they stuck with me for decades. It seems that as a woman, I am especially inundated with opinions about who I am and who I should be. I absorbed it from parents, friends, and community. When I wrote this story, I imagined the 'pop' of Kira's bubble as she stretched out wide and strong. It was a powerful feeling!

Mermaids symbolize beauty and sexual power. They also are symbols of independence and freedom.

1. What messages have you absorbed from others? Which are positive? Which are true? Which are negative? Which are false?

2. Are there any parts of your life that are encased in a bubble? Are you ready to pop that bubble? If not, what needs to happen so that you are?

Always Leaving, But Never Gone

I played the clarinet in high school. When Cher started her musician series, I said, "Be sure to include a clarinet!" So she painted this with me in mind. I own the original, of course. It's been an especially popular print. I'm sure it's because it's a portrait of me. :)

Clarinet trivia: 'Licorice stick' is slang for clarinet. If you dream of playing the clarinet, it means change is coming, and it's time to rid yourself of unhealthy relationships. If you actually play the clarinet, it means you are too cool for words. I'm just sayin'...

1. Is there such a thing as a healthy relationship, or all are relationships a wet mess? Where do you draw the line?

2. When is the last time you got up and just danced to the music? I challenge you to do it RIGHT NOW. Especially if you're in a group. Remember how much fun it was to dance with your besties?

What Dreams Are Left

I wrote this piece while sitting on a bench at Mt. Angel Abbey in Oregon. I gazed across the Willamette Valley to the Coast Range, and thought about its history. The Coast Range formed as the North American plate moved over the same magma pockets that created the current Cascade Range. As the plate continued to move, the Coast Range was eventually severed from its volcanic roots. The day I sat there, I felt as old as those mountains, and I wanted to sit on the bench forever.

1. Do you ever have times when you want to sit in solitude for a long, LONG time? Do you?

2. Do women encourage each other to take rest times? Do we support or compete with one another?

Dragonfly Dreams

After thirty years of living in Salem, Oregon, I moved to Portland for a year. It was the fulfillment of a dream. I found a cute little basement apartment that overlooked a pond and a creek. The week I moved in, I saw a red dragonfly flittering across the water. I didn't know there were red dragonflies! I sat right down and wrote this story, then asked Cher to do a painting of a red dragonfly. And THAT gave us the idea to create a book. A story about dreams gave rise to this dream. Fitting, yes?

Dragonflies do, in fact, have eyes with 30,000 lenses. They are favorite snacks of owls and bats. As a totem, the dragonfly stands for change, transformation, lightness of being, and being able to see both illusion and possibility. They call us to experience ourselves and the world in new ways.

1. Take a piece of paper and a pen. Don't think. Just start writing down dreams, no matter how foolish, small, or large they seem. Don't edit yourself. Write them all. When you've finished, review the list (WITHOUT judgment. It's not your job to toss them aside or criticize them, not yet.) Is there a theme to your dreams? What does that say to you?

2. Does one dream leap off the page? What will it cost to pursue that dream? What will it cost if you don't?

Woven Words

This painting hangs above my altar, a reminder that we are star stuff. (Be sure to check out Cher's web page and get your own Cher original. www.chertheart.com.) We don't have to reach for the heavens, we ARE the heavens. The Divine dwells within. The same is true of those around me, and this painting reminds me to honor the Divine within them, as well.

In Tarot, the Star represents hope shining forth in darkness. The light of the Star shines on the world, giving us a different perspective and the courage for creative transformation.

1. When words well up within you, do you squelch them or do they flow forth? How are they received?

2. How do you honor the Divine in others, especially those you find annoying?

ilmishmish

My grandparents emigrated from Syria/Lebanon in the early twentieth century. I loved the names of my Situ and her sisters: Aniese (ah-nee'-see), Jamilie (jah-mee'-lee) and Latifeh (lah-tee'-feh). They were nothing like the women in this story, but I wanted to use their beautiful names!

I loved creating these characters. It's so easy to look at the images in Cher's painting and imagine that they are all the same, but their internal lives couldn't be more different. Yet dig down another layer and underneath all the difference we once again find unity - the unity of all creation.

1. Do we see the grocery clerk, the baker, the restaurant server? What would our lives be like if we took the time to know - at least a little - every person with whom we have contact?

2. What is our responsibility, if any, to those who are unkind to us?

The Garden

This is my retelling of the second Biblical creation story. (Did you know there are two different stories? Check out Genesis 1 and then Genesis 2.) I've always found it amusing. The original story goes something like this: God created this beautiful garden, set Adam and Eve in it, then warned them against ONE tree. A serpent came and convinced Eve to take a bite of its fruit. It was an enlightening experience, which she shared with Adam.

Then God came for a visit. Adam ran and hid in the bushes, When God found him, Adam immediately tried to deflect responsibility. "Hey, it was that woman. That woman you gave me. Yeah, that's it - it's your fault. It's her fault."

I don't know. It reads like a comedy to me.

The Biblical account seemed a little biased, and I wondered what the story would look like from Eve's perspective. Some may think it's a little biased in a different direction now. :)

What's with the harp? Actually, it was serendipity. I loved Cher's image and felt strongly that it went with my retelling of the Adam & Eve fable, so I amended my story to include a harp. Then I looked into the symbolism of harps. Turns out, they represent a link between heaven and earth. Ancient people thought harps were mystical ladders into the spirit world. That's why angels are often depicted carrying a harp, and that's why harps represent communication with the divine.

1. What are your favorite stories, religious or otherwise? How do they shape how you view the world?

2. Every culture has 'identity stories' – fables that inform people's perceptions of themselves and the world. If we want to change our culture, is it as simple as changing our stories? Why or why not?

Birdie Whispers

Gossip. We all profess to hate it, but it can be SO enticing. I confess to occasionally succumbing to the allure of Birdie whispers. I confess to (rarely) BEING Birdie, though I resist, because I don't want to add to ill feelings in the world. I want to be an agent of peace. But sometimes, when it's someone with whom I struggle...

1. When, if ever, is gossip justified?

2. Do you believe we create the world by what we speak? How does that affect our responsibility for our words?

Clandestine Love

I wrote this originally as a poem for my MFA program. It started when I observed a tall weed dancing in the wind at the edge of an otherwise manicured lawn. How had it been overlooked? As I wrote about this misplaced nuisance, it morphed into a euphemism for furtive love. Cher's painting seemed the perfect accompaniment.

1. Have you ever loved someone or something that you (or others) felt was somehow inappropriate?

2. What types of love – between what types of people – do you feel is improper? Why?

Single-Fingered Salute

One afternoon, I sat at a pub on Hawthorne Street, sipping writer's fluid and watching women hurry in and out of a yarn store across the busy boulevard. Knitting has become a 'thing' amongst young women in Portland.

I always thought knitting was supposed to be a relaxing hobby, but these women barreled in and out of that store like the place was on fire. Career, check. Kid's tai chi, check. Knitting, check. The juxtaposition of their frantic scurrying and my relaxation on this weekday afternoon struck me as ironic.

1. Do you approach hobbies in a leisurely way or as another activity to ferociously tackle? Does your approach rejuvenate or drain you?

2. How do you feel when you see a working-age person relaxing in the middle of the day?

Amphibious Perspective

Domestic oppression is seen in all cultures and economic strata. It's present in the backhanded 'compliment', the disparaging comment, the raised voice, the veiled threat. We can recognize it in a person's self-blame, nervousness or desire to escape.

After I wrote this, I sent the story to Cher. "I'm sorry," I said, "it's a light-hearted painting, I don't know why a troubled story emerged. Shall I try again?"

"No," she replied. "It's perfect."

1. Where is the line between interfering in a relationship vs. calling out unacceptable behavior?

2. Are there behaviors you tolerate that perhaps you should not? What do you choose to do about it?

Desert Mother

I was so shy as a little girl. I would hide behind my mother's skirts. She would pull me out and tell me to go kiss Auntie or Uncle hello. The clear message was that my behavior embarrassed and shamed the family. So I learned to be social, to interact in ways that showed enjoyment. But inwardly, I was miserable.

The social face carried me through my adult years. "You're such an extrovert!" people would say. Little did they know how off-center and stressed I felt. In the past few years, I've embraced my inner hermit, and I'm much happier. I love my friends and I love our social activities. I also love solitary space, and I no longer apologize for taking time - lots of it - by myself.

1 Where do you fall on the introvert/extrovert spectrum? What invigorates and nurtures you? What things might you change/improve to better honor yourself?

2 'A desert in the ocean' in Celtic thought is that place where we can commune with the divine. It is the place where we find our life's purpose and enter into it. Have you found your desert in the ocean? Do you know your life's purpose?

All Together Now

Cher and I met on MySpace back in the 00's. We were both artists. Widows. Mothers of three. We clicked immediately.

We encourage each other and occasionally admonish, especially when one puts on dark glasses and proclaims to the other that the world looks grim. These stories and paintings do the same. They're a reminder that we are what we tell ourselves, we are what we see. This painting in particular is what I wish my reality to be.

1 Make a list of your friends and acquaintances. List them all. Now, place a star beside those who are supportive and encouraging. Put an X beside those who, in love, are willing to tell you hard truths. Make a new list of those whose names have both. What would your life look like if you concentrated on these people?

2 Is the list large enough? Small enough? If not, what will you do?